Boudicca: Warrior Queen
Thomas Jerome Baker

Statue of Queen Boudicca on the Thames River in London

Copyright © 2013 Thomas Jerome Baker
All rights reserved.
ISBN-13: 978-1494275617
ISBN-10: 1494275619

DEDICATION

"If you can dream, and not make dreams your master . . ."
~ Kipling

When I think of all the great women in my life, this book is the most appropriate place to dedicate words of gratitude to them, collectively, for all they have done for me. They will forgive me if I do not try to name them, for they are countless. I would surely omit someone of importance.

I would rather take the time to say to the women in my family, extended family, Chilean family as well as North American family, that I am the man I am today, thanks to you. It was you who taught me to dream big dreams, and to be relentless in pursuing my dreams.

It was you who taught me the power of perseverance. It was you who ensured my self-confidence would always be at a high level. You taught me to believe.

Indeed, as Kipling so eloquently says, in his poem, "**IF**":

> If you can talk with crowds and keep your virtue,
> Or walk with Kings—nor lose the common touch,
> If neither foes nor loving friends can hurt you,
> If all men count with you, but none too much;
> If you can fill the unforgiving minute
> With sixty seconds' worth of distance run,
> Yours is the Earth and everything that's in it,
> And—which is more—you'll be a Man, my son!

TABLE OF CONTENTS

Prologue .... Page 8

Chapter 1 A Fateful Decision ………….............…….. 10

Chapter 2 Queen Boudicca's Dream ……..…..……..... 13

Chapter 3 The Druids …………………….………… 17

Chapter 4 Attacked On The Isle Of Mona …..………... 22

Chapter 5 Boudicca's Revenge ………….…….…...... 26

Chapter 6 General Suetonius & the 14th Legion ……..... 29

Chapter 7 Counterattack Preparations …..….………... 33

Chapter 8 Queen Boudicaa Addresses The Celtics …...... 34

Chapter 9 General Suetonius Addresses The Romans … 36

Chapter 10 The Final Battle ...……..…….………….. 38

Epilogue ………………………….….................…… 41

ROMANUS ITE DOMUM …………….…......…….… 42

About The Author 43

ACKNOWLEDGMENTS

This book is because of my wife, Gabriela, and my son, Thomas Jerome Baker, Jr. I owe you both an absolute debt of gratitude for your inspiration.

It is you two who provide the impetus for me to write, again, and yet again. Thank you. I love you both more than words will ever express.

PROLOGUE

What is deemed as "history" is often determined by those who survived to write it. In other words, history is written by the victors. The Roman historian, Tacitus, left us an account of the Roman victory over Queen Boudicca in the year A.D. 60-61.

Boudicca was the queen of the Iceni of the East of England. She headed a rebellion against the occupying Romans in Britain in A.D. 60 in which seventy thousand Romans were killed. However, the rebellion was eventually crushed, and Boudicca committed suicide.

Prasutagus, the wealthy King of the Iceni tribe, had died. Upon his death, his wife, Queen Boudicca, became the new ruler of the Iceni tribe. She headed a rebellion against the occupying Romans in Britain in A.D. 60 in which more than seventy thousand Romans were killed. The rebellion was eventually crushed and Boudicca committed suicide. So, this is a neat, sweet ***his-story*** with a happy ending, if you were on the Roman side, that is.

Yet undeniably, every community has a memory of itself. Not a history, nor an archive, nor an authoritative record, but a ***living memory***, an awareness of a collective identity woven of a thousand stories.

Now, with the help of the Roman historian Tacitus, I shall tell you Queen Boudicca's story, ***her-story***……

Chapter 1 – A Fateful Decision

Queen Boudicca was a remarkably striking woman. Tacitus tells us that she was very tall, the glance of her eye most fierce; and her voice extremely harsh. Her hair was as red as a brightly burning fire. A great mass of her long, red hair fell down to her hips. Her appearance was absolutely terrifying.

In his will, King Prasutagus left equal shares of his considerable wealth for the Emperor of Rome and his two daughters. In this way he hoped to gain peace and tranquility for his kingdom and also provide for his family. Peace, tranquility and prosperity did not come to pass for neither his kingdom nor his family, in spite of his clever plan. Queen Boudicca, the new ruler of the Iceni tribe, decided *not* to honor King Prasutagus' will. She adamantly refused to give half of the wealth of her kingdom to the Roman Emperor, who was Nero Claudius Caesar Augustus Germanicus.

Now, King Prasutagus had always been friendly with the Romans. He paid taxes to Emperor Nero. In return, Nero let him rule the Iceni kingdom without interference from the Romans who were occupying Britain. This mutually beneficial relationship had allowed Prasutagus to amass considerable wealth over the course of a long, thirteen-year reign as King of the Iceni tribe. Emperor Nero wanted the new leader of the Iceni to continue to pay taxes to Rome. He was angered and offended by Queen Boudicca's refusal to pay. To punish her, he demanded that she pay higher taxes *and* give up the throne!

Paulinus Suetonius, a military officer of distinguished merit, was the Roman commander in Britain. His ambition was to become a famous commander.

Suetonius was well liked by the Roman people. This fact fueled his personal ambitions even more. By subduing the Iceni he hoped to achieve his goal of personal glory and fame. He knew he would gain favor with Emperor Nero if he resolved the problem of Queen Boudicca by removing her from the throne and taking the wealth of her kingdom for Rome. So, he decided to attack the Isle of Mona where Queen Boudicca was at. The Iceni were about to become a subject population…..

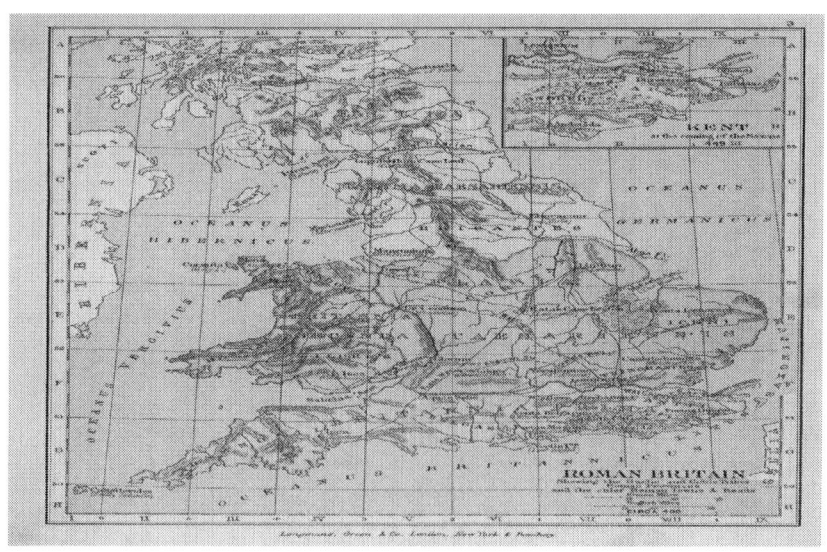

Chapter 2 – Queen Boudicca's Dream

Queen Boudicca awoke in the early morning. Here on the Isle of Mona the mornings were misty and magical. It was a place where the spirits walked the Earth and talked to those who needed counsel. Queen Boudicca opened her eyes but did not rise from her bed. Again she had dreamed of her beloved husband, King Prasutagus. For the past fortnight he had been visiting her dreams. He told her of his despair and his hope for his people, the Iceni Celtic tribe. Boudicca remembered his words of the past night clearly. Even now they reverberated in her mind, for he had spoken of the Iceni Kings of yesteryear.

"You are a member of the royal Iceni ruling pantheon," said Prasutagus. In the dream she sat quietly at his feet, listening attentively to her wise husband.

"Please tell me about the pantheon," she said.

"King Anted ruled during the time of the Roman invasion of 43 AD, but did not allow the tribe to defend our territory against the Romans", he said.

"What did he gain by doing that?" asked Queen Boudicca.

Prasutagus responded. "For this he was rewarded by being allowed to stay as ruler of the Iceni in the capacity of a *Client King*. He produced his first coins marked 'ANTED' to record his actions. The Iceni people were opposed to the rule of a leader who had no powers to govern his own people, and this prompted **Antedio** to issue coins inscribed 'ICENI', representing the name of the tribe. There was a fear that the name of 'Iceni' would disappear entirely. However, at least two of the Iceni aristocracy, **Aesu**-- and

Saenu-- produced their own coins around 45AD", said Prasatagus.

"Apparently Antedio, Aesu and Saenu were not content with the Roman power over our people", said Queen Boudicca.

"You are correct", said Prasatagus. "During the Iceni Civil War of 47AD, **Anted** was believed to have been killed and it was the Romans under the governor's son, Marcus Ostorius, who restored order. To ensure that peace remained, I was made Client King", said Prasatagus.

"I became Queen of the Iceni when you married me", said Boudicca.

"Yes, and then our two daughters were born", said Prasatagus.

He continued speaking. "**Aesu** was a friend of Anted, and a co-ruler of the Iceni with Anted, during the invasion of 43AD. He represented a rival faction within the Iceni who were opposed to the appointment by Rome of a single Client King. This was because he would lose all his powers to Anted. Aesu issued his own coins around 45AD, and was joined in this show of defiance by another Iceni leader, **Saenu**, who also issued coins while Anted was Client King", said Prasatagus.

"Aesu's and Saenu's coins were in defiance of Roman rule", said Boudicca. "What did the Romans do about this?" she asked.

"In 47AD, the Iceni, led by Aesu, Anted and Saenu, took the opportunity of a change in governorship to rebel against the Romans. All three Icenian nobles died during the fighting or were executed on the orders of Marcus Ostorius.

"So, when you were made Client King you accepted Roman rule and paid taxes to Emperor Nero", she said. "The Iceni people had peace and tranquility while you were king. For thirteen years there have been no wars with the Romans and you became a wealthy man. But the Iceni people were not free. A life without freedom is not worth living!" she exclaimed.

Chapter 3 – The Druids

Queen Boudicca arose from her bed. Her two daughters continued to sleep soundly. She moved quietly, so as not to awaken them. She wanted to speak to Alriada, the Druid soothsayer, about her dreams of the previous fortnight. Boudicca did not believe that Roman rule over the Iceni people was acceptable if it meant the loss of freedom for her people. She also did not think that the Romans had a right to the wealth of the Iceni people either. Surely Alriada would be able to help her understand the significance of her dreams and her feelings about freedom for the Iceni people of Britain.

Now, the Druids enjoyed a position of high status within the Iceni society. Historians tell us that they were a class apart from the warriors in Iceni society. They served the tribe as judges, prophets, soothsayers, wise men and as keepers of the collective memory. They used stories and songs to record the history of the Iceni. There were no written records. The Iceni Druids were the intellectuals in the Iceni warrior society.

We are told that the word 'druid' is thought to derive from the Greek *drus* (oak) and the Indo-European *wid* (wisdom), "which produces the apparent absurdity of 'oak-knower'. In any case, druids are typically associated with oak trees. Some say they held assemblies in sacred groves, that they prized the mistletoe growing on the oaks, or that they worshipped the trees themselves.

As Queen Boudicca approached the hut where Alriada the Druid dwelled she saw that Alriada was sitting under an oak tree. Alriada had already prepared a small area with stone tablets placed around it in a circular fashion. She appeared to be meditating. Her eyes were closed and she was chanting in a rhythmic voice that seemed to flow on and on with the gentle, morning breeze, taking flight over the ocean and returning to caress her soul. Alriada's voice reached out and found Queen Boudicca's inner ear.

"I have been waiting for you", said Alriada. "Sit down under the oak tree with me". Alriada indicated a place next to her where the circle of stones would be plainly visible to Queen Boudicca.

Wordlessly, Queen Boudicca did as Alriada had asked her to do. Alriada indicated the circle of stones to her. "Your future is there within the sacred circle if you have eyes to see it with", said Alriada.

Queen Boudicca never had a chance to see within the circle of stones. Loud shouts and drum beats averted her gaze. Pandemonium had broken out. Iceni warriors were running with their spears and clubs. Children were crying. Mothers were screaming. Dogs were barking. Above the din and commotion Queen Boudicca made out the cause of the pandemonium. Roman soldiers were attacking the Isle of Mona! Queen Boudicca ran swiftly to get her spear and sword to fight the Roman soldiers.

Meanwhile, Alriada the Druid, continued to sit under the oak tree. In the circle of stones before her she could clearly see the complete future of Boudicca, the Iceni Warrior Queen. She watched the events in Queen Boudicca's life take form and play out before her wise, all-knowing eyes. The events stretched even further than the life of Boudicca. What we do in life echoes in eternity, shaping the future of those who are as yet unborn. The final event visible to Alriada the Druid was Emperor Magnus Clemens Maximus, (better known in Wales as King Macsen Wledig), withdrawing the Romans from Britain. It was the year…..

Chapter 4 – Attacked On the Isle Of Mona

The account given by Tacitus of the attack by the Romans reads like Julius Ceaser. "Vini. Vidi. Vici." I CAME. I SAW. I CONQUERED. It was a massacre.

What did Queen Boudicca see when she rushed out to meet the Romans in battle? She saw Roman soldiers in formation, ready for battle but frozen in stupefied terror at the sight of the Inceni warriors.

Queen Boudicca tells **_her-story_** of that day: "We were prepared to fight to the death. Women were running through the ranks of our warriors looking for their children. Most of us were dressed in our black sleeping attire which is worn in the night on this mystical spirit island. Our hair was loose and blown by the wind. Flaming torches taken from the morning cooking fires were held in our hands. The frantic rage of the Furies was on every face. Although we had been taken by surprise the dawning day would not go by without our glorious warriors fighting to the death. The Druids were ranged in order, with hands uplifted, invoking the gods, and pouring forth horrible incantations of doom. The Romans were terrified. In the Roman soldiers' faces you could see their fear, terror and paralysis. They stood in stupid amazement, as if their limbs were no longer under their control."

Queen Boudicca took a breath and continued **her-story**: "The Roman General, Suetonius, exhorted his soldiers. He said to them…."

"Hold the line!" shouted General Suetonius. "Hold your ground! Stay with me!" "You see before you women and fanatical priests! YOU ARE ROMAN SOLDIERS! This Legion will NOT be disgraced by the likes of such! I see in your eyes that same fear that would take the hearts of men. The day may come when the courage of men fails. But it is NOT this day! This day we FIGHT!"

Queen Boudicca continued: "General Suetonius rallied his men. They were diffused with new vigor. The men shouted out their battle cry and rushed forward on line with General Suetonius leading them into battle. Our warriors fought valiantly, but we were no match for the inspired Roman soldiers. We were defeated quickly. The

Romans immediately destroyed the religious oak tree groves of our Druids." "But that is not all", she said quietly. "They were not content with taking the island of Mona and destroying the sacred oak groves. General Suetonius had me publicly flogged and my two daughters were violated by Roman soldiers." Queen Boudicca was silent, unable to speak. She could not contain her tears at the remembrance of that infamous day. She wept. After a while, she continued. "The other Iceni chiefs on the island suffered in a like manner and their families were treated like slaves. It was a horrible humiliation and I will get revenge for the atrocities committed to me, my daughters and my people by the Romans! This I swear by all that is sacred to me, Boudicca, wife of King Prasutagus, Queen of the Iceni Celts!"

Chapter 5 – Boudicca's Revenge

General Suetonius had allowed the humiliated and disgraced Queen Boudicca and her daughters to return to her Iceni tribe in the East of Britain. Her continued presence on The Isle of Mona was undesirable. While General Suetonius was employed in making his arrangements to secure the island, he received intelligence that Britain had revolted, and that the whole province was up in arms.

Queen Boudicca had sworn to avenge her treatment at the hands of the Romans. When she returned she instigated a rebellion within her tribe and persuaded the Trinovantes tribe directly to the south to join her. The Trinobantians joined in the revolt. The Romano-British towns of Camulodunum (Colchester), Verulamium (St.

Albans) and Londinium (London) were selected for attack by Queen Boudicca.

Camulodunum was the first town to be attacked. Before the attack Queen Boudicca wanted a sign that her plans would be favored with success. "Bring Alriada the Druid to me", she ordered.

"I am here by your side", said Alriada. "I knew you would seek me out this night". "Come with me".

Alriada took her to a vantage point where she could see the River Thames below. "Behold the river", said Alriada. "Tell me what you see".

"Nothing, said Queen Boudicca. "I see nothing". Suddenly the river Thames began to transform itself. She saw the image of a colony in ruins in the transparent water;

the river was purple with blood, and, at the tide of ebb, the figures of human bodies were traced in the sand.

"Victory", said Queen Boudicca. "It is to be a great victory for the Celtic people, is it not?" she asked. She turned to look at Alriada the Druid, but she had disappeared into the mist of the night. Queen Boudicca was alone.

The town was attacked but managed to hold out for two days. Finally it was taken by Queen Boudicca's Celtic warriors. The town was pillaged and burned. The streets ran red with Roman blood.

General Petilius Cerealis, who commanded the Roman ninth legion, marched to the relief of the town. Queen Boudicca's warriors advanced to do battle with the ninth legion. The legion was defeated and routed. The infantry was mercilessly cut to pieces. General Cerealis escaped only with his cavalry. Catus Decianus, the Procurator of the province, became alarmed at the scene of carnage which he saw all around him. Dreading the indignation and retribution of the Celtic people, whom by force, coercion and oppression he had driven to despair, escaped and crossed over into Gaul.

Chapter 6 – General Suetonius and the 14th Legion

Where was General Suetonius while all this was going on? He had first gotten word about Queen Boudicca's rebellion while he was still building a Roman garrison on the Isle of Mona. He knew his forces would be needed to put down the rebellion and therefore had begun to march his soldiers to Londinium. Would he arrive in time to help that town?

Suetonius, undismayed by the disaster of the 9th Legion, marched through the heart of the country as far as Londinium. It was not yet a colony, but the chief residence of merchants, and the great center of trade and commerce. In Londinium he planned to defeat Queen Boudicca. However, the small numbers of his little army, and the fate of General Cerealis made him reconsider his plan. He decided to leave Londinium because he believed by doing so he could secure the rest of the province. He had no doubts that Queen Boudicca would want to take this town. General Suetonius wanted to avoid a battle with her forces at this time. Neither supplications, nor the tears of the inhabitants could induce him to change his plan. The signal for the march was given. All who chose to follow his banners were taken under his protection. Of all who, on account of their advanced age, the weakness of their sex, of the attractions of the situation, thought proper to remain behind, not one escaped the fury and the rage of Queen Boudicca and her Celtic warriors.

Queen Boudicca tells us **her-story** about the destruction of Londinium: "The town of Londinium lay before us. It was quiet in the town. We had expected the Romans to fight us here. Cautiously we entered, expecting a trap. At any moment we expected the Roman soldiers to come out of hiding to fight us. They never did. They had left the town undefended. My warriors pillaged, plundered, and burned Londinium to the ground. No one was left alive. We put Londinium to the sword and to the torch. It was another great victory for my people. We were united, one people, Celtic warriors. As such we were invincible".

Queen Boudica continued to tell **her-story**. "The inhabitants of Verulamium, a municipal town, were in like manner put to the sword and to the torch. Again, no one was left alive in the town. The sky was black with the smoke from the fires within the city. Soon we will force the Roman invaders from our country. The Celtics will be free. The Roman Army will not fight us. Their generals seek only to avoid us in battle. We pillage and plunder their towns. We are invincible!" she said. "I am Queen Boudicca, the Warrior Queen of the Celtics! I will have my revenge and force the Romans to leave Britain!"

The Roman historian Tacitus tells us that no less than seventy thousand people, all citizens or allies of Rome, were killed. Not a single prisoner of war was taken. Queen Boudicca had extracted a horrible revenge on the

Romans for the humiliation she suffered at the Isle of Mona.

Chapter 7- Counterattack Preparations

The 14th Legion, with the veterans of the 20th Legion, joined General Suetonius. He now had ten thousand men in his army. He now felt ready to fight a decisive battle. He chose a place surrounded by woods, narrow at the entrance, and sheltered in the rear by a thick forest. He would not be attacked from the rear. He knew the enemy could only approach from the front. An open plain lay before him. He drew up his men in the following order: the legions in close array formed the center; the lightly armed troops were stationed at hand to serve as occasion might require: the cavalry took post in the wings. He knew the Celtics would fight in an undisciplined multitude with no organization. They would shout, curse, scream their battle cry and charge. There would be no regular battle line formed. The Celtics would be sure of victory. They would even place their wives in wagons at the extremity of the plain, where they might survey the scene of action, and behold the wonders of Celtic warriors in action.

General Suetonius wondered aloud to himself: "Would his tactics prove superior to the sheer numbers of the Celtics?" He knew he was betting his life on the answer to that question. Queen Boudicca would not spare his life……

Chapter 8 – Queen Boudicaa Addresses The Celtics

So it came to pass that the Celtics were prepared to do battle with General Suetonius Paullinus' Roman forces near Manduessedum in the Midlands. Queen Boudicca, in a chariot, with her two daughters before her, drove through the ranks of Celtic warriors. She tells us **her-story.** "This," she said, "is not the first time that the Celtics have been led to battle by a woman. I have not come to boast the pride of a long line of ancestry, nor even to recover my kingdom and the stolen wealth of my family. I take the battlefield, like the meanest among you, to assert the cause of Celtic liberty, and to seek revenge for what was done to me at the Isle of Mona. My body and soul was left marked forever by the Roman lash of oppression. My two daughters were infamously violated by Roman cowards. From the pride and arrogance of the Roman nothing is sacred; all of us are subject to violation; the old endure the lash, and our virgins are deflowered. But the vindictive gods are now at hand. A Roman legion dared once to face the fury and might of the Celtic nation: with their lives they paid for their stupidity; those who survived the carnage of that day, lie poorly hid behind their entrenchments, meditating nothing but how to save themselves by disgraceful flight. It is a good day for Romans to die today. From the sounds of our preparations, and the shouts of the Celtic army, the Romans, even now, shrink back with terror. What will be their case when the assault begins? Look around, and view your numbers. Behold the proud display of warlike spirits, and consider the motives for which we draw the avenging sword. TODAY WE MUST EITHER CONQUER, OR DIE WITH GLORY. There is no alternative. Though a WOMAN, my resolution is fixed: the MEN, if they please, may survive with infamy, and live in bondage."

"CONQUER OR DIE!!"

Chapter 9 – General Suetonius Addresses The Romans

General Suetonius, in a moment of such importance, did not remain silent. He expected every thing from the valor of his men, and yet knew he would have to inspire and animate them to the attack.

"Despise them," he said. "The savage uproar, the yells and shouts are from undisciplined Barbarians. There are more women than men among them. They are void of spirit and supplied with inferior weapons. They are not soldiers who come to offer battle; they are bastards, runaways, the refuse of your swords, who have often fled before you, and will again take flight when they see the conqueror flaming in the ranks of war. In all engagements it is the courage of a few that turns the fortune of the day. It will be your immortal glory, that so few Roman soldiers can equal the exploits of a great and powerful army. Keep your ranks; discharge your javelins; rush forward to a close attack; bear down all with your bucklers, and cut a passage with your swords. Pursue the vanquished, and never think of spoil and plunder. Conquer, Conquer, Conquer! Victory gives you everything. Victory! Victory! Victory!"

With that a great roar went up from the soldiers. They were ready to live and die for Rome. It was a good day for Celtic warriors to die on the battlefield.

General Suetonius, anticipating the victory, gave the signal for the charge. "SOLDIERS OF ROME, C-H-A-R-G-E!!!" he yelled.

Chapter 10 – The Final Battle

The battle began. The Roman Legion presented a close, organized battle line. The narrow entrance gave them shelter on their sides. The Celtics advanced ferociously. They used their weapons randomly. In that instant, the Romans rushed forward in the form of a wedge. The lightly armed reinforcements followed with equal passion. The cavalry, at the same time, bore down upon the enemy, and, with their spears, overpowered all who dared to make a stand before them. The Celtic warriors took to flight, but their wagons in the rear obstructed their passage. A dreadful slaughter followed. No one was spared by the Romans. Neither male nor female. Neither young nor old was spared. The cattle and the horses and the dogs were not spared. The glory of the day was equal to the most splendid victory of ancient times. Eighty thousand Celtic men, women and children were put to the sword. The Romans lost about four hundred men, with another four hundred wounded.

What of Queen Boudicca? What does she do now? She tells us her final **heroic-story**:

"What great despair fills me for my vanquished people? We have lost all hope for freedom. My Celtic brothers, my Celtic sisters, my Celtic daughters even, lie dead and dying at my feet. If I am not to be free in life, then I choose the liberty of death! (She takes poison) "Oh sweet Death, bring your chariot to take me to a place where I and my people may be free! (*She falls to the ground, succumbing to the effects of the poison, dead.*)

Poenius Postumius, the Prefect in the camp of the 2nd Legion, as soon as he heard of the brave exploits of the 14th and 20th Legions, felt disgraced for not fighting. Stung with remorse, he fell upon his sword and expired.

THE END

Epilogue

This story is told in the "*Annals* of Tacitus", written about AD 110-120. Tacitus had a special interest in Britain because his father-in-law, Agricola, became governor of the Province in AD 77-85 after a successful military campaign in Wales and the north. This campaign, together with some details on the native Celtic tribes, is described in the book "*Agricola*" by Tacitus, written in AD 98.

After their defeat in AD 61, the Iceni were resettled in a civitas capital at Caistor-by-Norwich (also called Caistor St.Edmunds), located along the River Tas. The site may be visited today, along with related exhibits at the Norwich Museum.

(ROMANS GO HOME)

383AD – EMPEROR MAGNUS CLEMENS MAXIMUS

While the Goths are attacking Rome, Magnus Clemens Maximus a Roman governor, has taken advantage of the turmoil and made himself Emperor. Magnus takes many Roman troops from Britain in an attempt to seize Gaul and Spain.

399AD – ROMANS EVACUATE TROOPS

The Romans have started to evacuate troops from Britain. Reinforcements are desperately needed on the continent to protect Rome.

410 AD – PERMANENT TROOP WITHDRAWAL

In 410AD the Goths of the East sacked Rome and troops were *permanently* withdrawn from Britain to defend the collapsing Roman Empire.

ABOUT THE AUTHOR

Thomas Baker is the Past-President of TESOL Chile (2010-2011). He is the Coordinator of the English Department at Colegio Internacional SEK in Santiago, Chile.

He is the Co-Founder and Co-Organiser of EdCamp Santiago: free, participant-driven, democratic, conversation based professional development for teachers, by teachers. EdCamp Santiago 2013 was held at Universidad UCINF in Santiago.

Thomas is also a past member of the Advisory Board for the International Higher Education Teaching and Learning Association (HETL), where he also serves as a reviewer and as the HETL Ambassador for Chile.

http://goo.gl/qYo8BH

Thomas enjoys writing about a wide variety of topics. He has written the following genres: romance, historical fiction, autobiographical, sports history/biography, and English Language Teaching.

http://goo.gl/mdU4iG

http://www.profesorbaker.com

email: profesorbaker@gmail.com

Twitter: @profesortbaker

Printed in Great Britain
by Amazon